EARLY BIRD STORIES

The Smart Hat

Early ★ Reader

Lerner Publications Company
A division of Lerner Publishing Group, Inc.
241 First Avenue North
Minneapolis, MN 55401 USA

For reading levels and more information, look up this title at
www.lernerbooks.com.

Main body text set in Mikado a. Typeface provided by HVD Fonts.

Library of Congress Cataloging-in-Publication Data

Names: Jones, Cath, 1965– author. | Nicholls, Paul (Illustrator), illustrator.
Title: The smart hat / by Cath Jones ; illustrated by Paul Nicholls.
Description: First American edition. | Minneapolis : Lerner Publications, 2019. |
    Series: Early bird readers. Blue (Early bird stories).
Identifiers: LCCN 2018018051 (print) | LCCN 2018026032 (ebook) |
    ISBN 9781541543300 (eb pdf) | ISBN 9781541541726 (lb : alk. paper) |
    ISBN 9781541546141 (pb : alk. paper)
Subjects: LCSH: Readers—Animals. | Readers (Primary) | Animals—Juvenile
    literature.
Classification: LCC PE1127.A6 (ebook) | LCC PE1127.A6 J667 2019 (print) |
    DDC 428.6/2—dc23

LC record available at https://lccn.loc.gov/2018018051

Manufactured in the United States of America
1-45346-38996-8/1/2018

EARLY BIRD
STORIES

The Smart Hat

Cath Jones

Illustrated by
Paul Nicholls

Lerner Publications ◆ Minneapolis

The queen's bell was ringing.
Ding-dong.

The queen took a look in the big box.

She had such a shock!

The hat said,

"Too-wit-too-woo!"

"This is not my smart hat!"

said the queen.

The queen said,

"I need a smart hat now."

"I will be a hat," said Owl.

"Just for you!"

The owl sat down
on the queen's head.

"Wow!" said the crowd.

"Look at the queen's owl hat!"

"The hat can hoot!" said the crowd.

That night, the queen took
Owl to the park.

Owl went **zoom** into the dark night!

The next day the queen felt sad.

But then . . .

Ding-dong.

. . . she got a shock!

Quiz

1. That must be . . . ?
   a) My smart hat
   b) My smart dress
   c) My smart crown

2. What was in the box?
   a) A car
   b) A brown owl
   c) A hat

3. Where does the queen go with her owl hat?
   a) To the zoo
   b) To a shop
   c) To a park

4. What did the owl do?
a) Hoot
b) Dance
c) Sing

5. The next day the queen felt . . . ?
a) Sad
b) Happy
c) Angry

Leveled for Guided Reading

Early Bird Stories have been edited and leveled by leading educational consultants to correspond with guided reading levels. The levels are assigned by taking into account the content, language style, layout, and phonics used in each book.

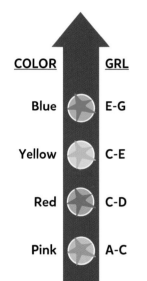

COLOR	GRL
Blue	E-G
Yellow	C-E
Red	C-D
Pink	A-C